TIME FOR KIDS®

DEVELOPING READER 2 · Science Scoops

P9-CLS-204

Frogs!

By the Editors of TIME FOR KIDS
WITH KATHRYN HOFFMAN SATTERFIELD

HarperCollins*Publishers*

About the Author: Kathryn Hoffman Satterfield is an editor at TIME FOR KIDS®. She has written numerous articles about animals, the environment, and social issues. She is also the author of the TIME FOR KIDS® biography BENJAMIN FRANKLIN.

To Sam, a prince who was never a frog, and my uncle Steve, who cares for creatures big and small.

Special thanks to Christopher J. Raxworthy, a biologist with the American Museum of Natural History's herpetology department. –K.H.S.

Frogs!
Copyright © 2006 by Time Inc.
Used under exclusive license by HarperCollins Publishers Inc.
Manufactured in China.
All rights reserved. No part of this book may be used or reproduced in any manner whatsoever without written permission except in the case of brief quotations embodied in critical articles and reviews. For information address HarperCollins Children's Books, a division of HarperCollins Publishers, 1350 Avenue of the Americas, New York, NY 10019.
www.harperchildrens.com

Library of Congress Cataloging-in-Publication Data is available.

ISBN-10: 0-06-078221-8 (pbk.) — ISBN-10: 0-06-078222-6 (trade)
ISBN-13: 978-0-06-078221-4 (pbk.) — ISBN-13: 978-0-06-078222-1 (trade)

6 7 8 9 10
First Edition

Copyright © by Time Inc.
TIME FOR KIDS and the Red Border Design are Trademarks of Time Inc. used under license.

Photography and Illustration Credits:
Cover: Marian Bacon—Animals Animals; cover inset: Ken Griffiths—NHPA; cover front flap: James Carmichael, Jr.—NHPA; title page: Marian Bacon—Animals Animals; pp. 4–5: Carol Buchanan—Alamy; pp. 6–7: Lynda Richardson—Corbis; pg. 7 (inset): Gary Meszaros—Bruce Coleman; pp. 8–9: Anne Reas; pg. 9 (inset): Anne Reas; pp. 10–11: James Gerholdt—Peter Arnold, Inc.; pg. 10 (inset): Frans Lanting—Minden; pp. 12–13: Dante Fenolio—Photo Researchers; pp. 14–15: Michael & Patricia Fogden—Minden; pg. 15 (inset): Mark Moffett—Minden; pp. 16–17: Stephen Dalton—NHPA; pp. 18–19: T. Kitchin & V. Hurst—NHPA; pg. 19 (inset): Anne Reas; pp. 20–21: Stephen Dalton—NHPA; pp. 22–23: Art Wolfe—Photo Researchers; pp. 24–25: Gail M. Shumway—Bruce Coleman; pp. 26–27: Paul Freed—Animals Animals; pp. 28–29: Takeshi Ebinuma; pg. 29 (inset): Benno Friedman—Time Life Pictures/Getty Images; pp. 30–31: Stephen Dalton—Animals Animals; pg. 30 (inset): Nigel J. Dennis—Gallo Images/Corbis; pg 32 (amphibian): Paul Freed—Animals Animals; pg. 32 (camouflage): Takeshi Ebinuma; pg. 32 (froglet): Stephen Dalton—NHPA; pg. 32 (habitat): Frans Lanting—Minden; pg. 32 (metamorphosis): Mark Moffett—Minden; pg. 32 (tadpole): Michael & Patricia Fogden—Minden; pg. 32 (fun fact): John Courtney

Acknowledgments:
For TIME FOR KIDS: Editorial Director: Keith Garton; Editor: Nelida Gonzalez Cutler; Art Director: Rachel Smith; Photography Editor: Jill Tatara

HarperCollins books may be purchased for educational, business, or sales promotional use. For information, please write: Special Markets Department, HarperCollins Publishers Inc., 10 East 53rd Street, New York, NY 10022.

 Check us out at www.timeforkids.com

CONTENTS

Bullfrog on
a lily pad

One Hoppy Family

Three red-eyed tree frogs, one with an inflated vocal sac

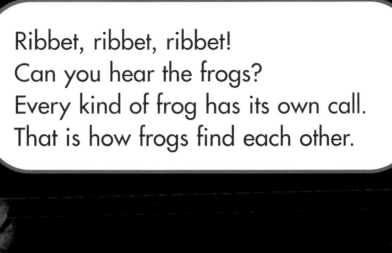

Ribbet, ribbet, ribbet!
Can you hear the frogs?
Every kind of frog has its own call.
That is how frogs find each other.

A bullfrog
in Virginia

Salamanders are amphibians too.

Frogs are amphibians.

Amphibians are animals with backbones
that live both on land and in the water.
Amphibians are cold-blooded.
Their body temperature changes when
the temperature around them changes.

Take a close look at a frog.

Frogs and toads look a lot alike. Sometimes even experts cannot tell them apart!

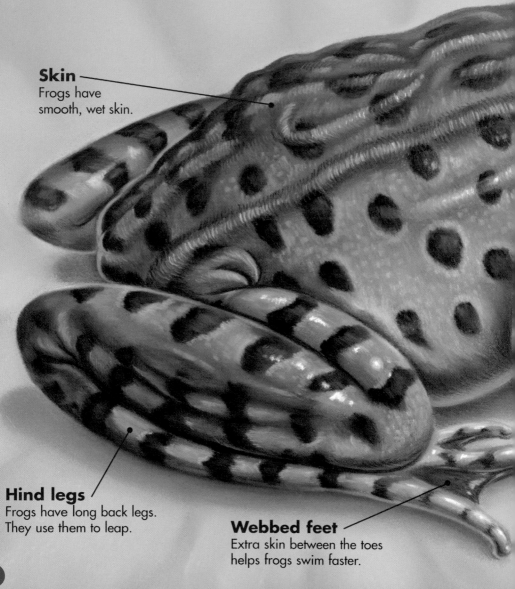

Skin
Frogs have smooth, wet skin.

Hind legs
Frogs have long back legs. They use them to leap.

Webbed feet
Extra skin between the toes helps frogs swim faster.

All toads are frogs.
Most toads live on land.
They usually have dry,
warty skin and short back legs.
There is little or no webbing
between their toes.

Eyes
Most frogs and toads
have bulging eyes.
They can see in front,
to the sides, and partly
behind them.

Tympanic membranes
Frogs and toads have eardrums
on the surface of their skin.
They have very good hearing.

Front legs
Frogs use their short front
legs to prop themselves up.

Desert spadefoot frog

African
clawed frog

Frogs live in many habitats.

Most frogs like to be wet.
They live near ponds, swamps, and lakes.
But some frogs live in the desert.
They go underground to stay cool and wet.

CHAPTER TWO

A Frog's Life

All frogs begin life as an egg.
Some frogs lay as many as
ten thousand eggs.
Most frogs do not protect their eggs.
But the male mountain coqui frog
keeps a close watch!

Male mountain
coqui frog with eggs

A tadpole hatches from a frog egg.
It has a long tail and gills, like a fish.
The tadpole swims, eats, and grows.
It goes through a change
called a metamorphosis.
Gradually the gills
disappear and lungs form.

**Red-eyed leaf frog
tadpoles in Costa Rica**

A male golden poison frog carrying tadpoles

**European frog
froglet**

The tadpole begins to look like a frog.
Its legs form and its tail shrinks.
At about twelve weeks old,
the tadpole becomes a froglet.
Soon its tail will disappear.

Strawberry poison
dart frogs

The planet is hopping with frogs!

Frogs can be green, gray, yellow, orange, red, or blue.
There are nearly five thousand kinds of frogs.
Scientists keep finding new species.

How Big?

The Cuban tree toad is one of the world's smallest frogs.
It only grows to half an inch long.

The Goliath frog is the world's largest frog.
It can grow up to fifteen inches long.
That's as big as a computer keyboard!

CHAPTER THREE

The Hungry Frog

White's tree frog

Some frogs eat spiders, snails, slugs, earthworms, and insects. They catch bugs with their long, sticky tongues. Frogs eat insects that can destroy farmers' crops.

Big frogs eat big meals.
They eat mice, small reptiles,
and even other frogs.
Frogs use their eyeballs to
swallow food.
By blinking, a frog pushes food
down its throat.

South American bullfrog
eating a walking stick

Some frogs have favorite foods.

The Madagascar mantella frog
mainly eats ants.
The ants contain poison.
This makes the frog's skin poisonous.

Madagascar
mantella frogs

CHAPTER FOUR

Are Frogs

Many frogs have poisonous skin.
The most poisonous frogs
are brightly colored.
This warns animals that these frogs
are not safe to eat.

in Trouble?

Blue poison
dart frogs

Some frogs use camouflage to protect themselves.
They blend into the trees, plants, or dirt where they live.
The Vietnamese mossy frog looks like a little clump of moss.

Vietnamese
mossy frog

Spotlight

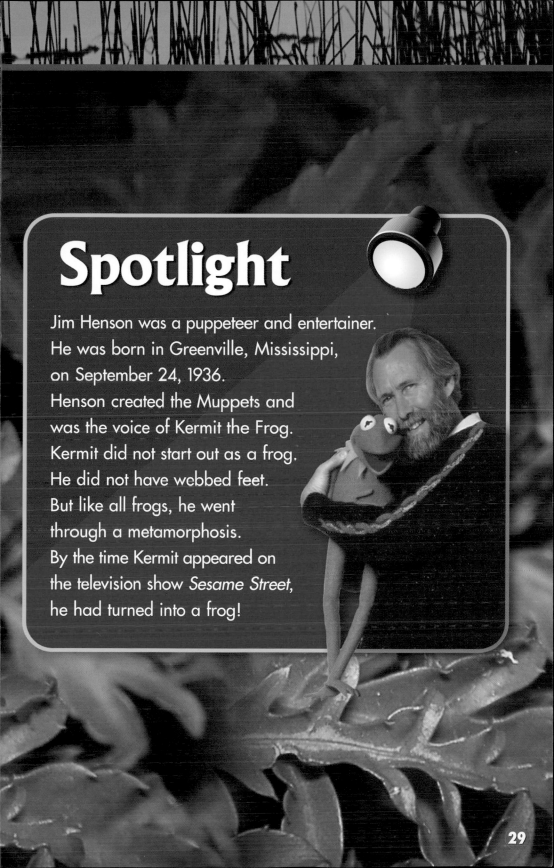

Jim Henson was a puppeteer and entertainer. He was born in Greenville, Mississippi, on September 24, 1936. Henson created the Muppets and was the voice of Kermit the Frog. Kermit did not start out as a frog. He did not have webbed feet. But like all frogs, he went through a metamorphosis. By the time Kermit appeared on the television show *Sesame Street*, he had turned into a frog!

Frog habitats are being destroyed.

When humans cut down trees,
some frogs have no place to live.
Pollution also hurts frogs.
Their thin skin can absorb harmful chemicals.
Many kinds of frogs are in danger of extinction.
Scientists are working hard to protect them.

An endangered tomato
frog from Madagascar

Wallace's flying frog

Did You Know?

- Flying frogs do not really fly. The webbing between their toes helps them glide from tree branch to branch.

- A golden poison frog contains enough poison to kill 20,000 mice.

- Some frogs can leap more than twenty times farther than the length of their body.

- The Senegal running frog does not jump. It runs through tall, grassy areas.

WORDS to Know

Amphibian: any cold-blooded animal that can live both on land and in water

Habitat: the place where an animal lives

Camouflage: to blend in with the surroundings

Metamorphosis: a change from an immature stage to an adult stage

Froglet: a young, small frog

Tadpole: a young frog that lives in the water and has a long tail and gills

FUN FACT

The wood frog can live in the extreme cold.
It can survive for weeks with more than half its body frozen.